RANA RATANSINGH, WHO RULED OVER KURKHI IN RAJASTHAN, WAS A GOOD RULER AND WAS LOVED BY HIS PEOPLE. HE HAD A BEAUTIFUL DAUGHTER NAMED **MIRA**.

ONE DAY WHEN MIRA WAS ABOUT FIVE YEARS OLD, A WEDDING PROCESSION PASSED BY THE PALACE.

MOTHER, WHERE IS MY BRIDEGROOM?

COME, I WILL TAKE YOU TO HIM.

HER MOTHER LED HER TO AN IMAGE OF LORD KRISHNA, KEPT IN A CORNER OF THE ROOM. MIRA LOVED THIS IMAGE.

THERE IS YOUR HUSBAND! GOPALA HIMSELF. LOVE HIM AND SERVE HIM AS A GOOD WIFE WOULD HER HUSBAND.

MIRA TOOK HER MOTHER SERIOUSLY.

FROM NOW ON GOPALA IS MINE AND I AM HIS.

FROM NOW ON YOU MUST PROTECT ME, FOR I AM YOUR BRIDE.

AND SHE LEFT OFF ALL OTHER PLAY.

SO THE YEARS PASSED AND MIRA WAS STEADFAST IN HER LOVE OF HER DIVINE HUSBAND.

ONE DAY A BRIDAL PROCESSION ARRIVED AND MIRA WAS MARRIED TO PRINCE BHOJRAJ OF CHITTOR WHO WAS KNOWN FOR HIS VALOUR AND HIS DEEP HATRED OF THE MUGHALS —

INDEED I AM FORTUNATE! MY PRINCESS IS THE MOST BEAUTIFUL GIRL I HAVE EVER SEEN.

MIRA WAS AN IDEAL HINDU WIFE...

...AND WAS LOVED BY HER HUSBAND.

BUT AS SOON AS HER HOUSEHOLD DUTIES WERE OVER, MIRA WOULD TURN TO HER DIVINE HUSBAND— HER GOPALA— WHOM SHE HAD BROUGHT WITH HER.

HER MOTHER-IN-LAW DID NOT APPROVE OF THIS.

DURGA IS OUR FAMILY GODDESS. YOU SHOULD WORSHIP HER!

MIRA WAS ADAMANT.

FORGIVE ME, MOTHER. I HAVE ALREADY OFFERED MYSELF TO LORD KRISHNA. I CANNOT BOW BEFORE ANY OTHER DEITY.

BHOJRAJ'S SISTER UDA ALSO TRIED HER HAND BUT IN VAIN.

GODDESS DURGA MAY BE OFFENDED AND MAY LAY A CURSE ON OUR HOUSEHOLD. WHY DON'T YOU YIELD?

FULL OF ANGER, SHE DECIDED TO TAKE REVENGE.

MIRA GOES EVERY EVENING TO THE TEMPLE. I WILL TELL MY BROTHER SHE HAS A LOVER!

A CLEVER IDEA.

UDA AND HER COMPANIONS WENT TO BHOJRAJ.

FORGIVE ME, BROTHER! HAVE YOU LOST THE LOVE OF YOUR WIFE? ARE YOU NOT MAN ENOUGH FOR HER? IT IS A SHAME THAT THE FAIR NAME OF CHITTOR AND YOURS SHOULD BE SULLIED BY THE CONDUCT OF YOUR WIFE.

MIRA UNFAITHFUL?? I CANNOT BELIEVE IT. LET ME SEE FOR MYSELF.

THAT NIGHT HE STOOD OUTSIDE THE TEMPLE DOOR, LISTENING CAREFULLY.

WHY DO YOU KEEP YOUR MIRA WAITING? ALL SHE WANTS IS TO BE ABLE TO LOVE YOU! SHE YEARNS ONLY FOR YOU.

DRAWING HIS SWORD, BHOJRAJ RUSHED INTO THE TEMPLE.

SHOW ME YOUR LOVER THAT I MAY KILL HIM!!

THERE HE IS! HE HAS STOLEN MY HEART AND WILL NOT GIVE IT BACK!

KING BHOJRAJ, CONVINCED THAT HIS WIFE WAS INSANE, DECIDED TO HUMOUR HER. HE BUILT A TEMPLE FOR HER WHERE SHE COULD WORSHIP HER STONE LOVER TO HER HEART'S CONTENT! SOON DEVOTEES FLOCKED AROUND HER AND SHE OFTEN SANG AND DANCED HERSELF INTO ECSTASIES OVER HER LORD.

MIRA'S LORD IS GOPALA! ♪

THE STORY OF MIRA'S DEVOTION TO LORD KRISHNA BY SONG, DANCE AND DISCOURSES SPREAD FAR AND WIDE. IT REACHED THE EARS OF THE MUGHAL EMPEROR AKBAR AND HIS COURT MUSICIAN, TANSEN.

TANSEN, I CANNOT REST TILL I HAVE HEARD THE DEVOTIONAL SONGS OF MIRABAI!!

YES, MY LORD. THE SONGS, THEY SAY, ARE SO DEEPLY DEVOTIONAL THAT THE LORD HIMSELF APPEARS. WE MUST FIND OUR WAY THERE!

KNOWING THAT THE RAJPUTS HATED THE MUGHALS, THEY DECIDED TO GO DISGUISED AS HINDUS.

THESE SAFFRON ROBES OF A SADHU ARE THE MOST SUITABLE.

YES, MY LORD.

AT LAST THEY REACHED THE TEMPLE WHERE MIRA SAT BEFORE HER LORD.

AS SOON AS THE DEVOTEES STARTED POURING IN, SHE BEGAN HER SINGING. SOME OF THEM JOINED HER, OTHERS LISTENED...

I, MIRA, SOLD MYSELF TO GOPALA EVERLASTINGLY— AND THEN FROM WORLDLINESS I PARTED COMPANY!

AT THE END OF THE DAY'S PRAYERS, AKBAR AND TANSEN WERE IN A TRANCE. AKBAR APPROACHED MIRA, TOUCHED HER FEET AND PLACED A NECKLACE AT THE FEET OF THE IMAGE.

IN THE NAME OF HIM— WHOM YOU ARE SO DEVOTED TO, ACCEPT MY HUMBLE GIFT.

I CANNOT BUT ACCEPT WHAT IS OFFERED IN HIS NAME.

AND THE EMPEROR LEFT THE PLACE WITH A HEAVY HEART.

MIRA'S SONGS HAVE FILLED MY HEART WITH A STRANGE PEACE! YET, I HOPELESSLY YEARN FOR MORE AND WILL ALWAYS DO SO!

NEWS LEAKED OUT THAT THE MUGHAL EMPEROR AND HIS MUSICIAN HAD VISITED MIRA.

THEY SAY, AKBAR THE MUGHAL TOUCHED THE FEET OF MIRA!

WHAT WILL OUR PRINCE SAY?

DOES HE KNOW?

WHEN RANA BHOJRAJ HEARD OF IT, HE SEETHED WITH ANGER. SANE OR INSANE HIS WIFE HAD DEGRADED HERSELF. HE SUMMONED HER.

DID YOU DARE ALLOW A MUGHAL CUR TO TOUCH YOUR FEET, THE FEET OF A RAJPUT PRINCESS? DID YOU DARE ALLOW HIM TO ENTER YOUR TEMPLE?

MIRA'S SERENE SILENCE ONLY MADE HIM MORE ANGRY.

FOR THE DISGRACE YOU HAVE BROUGHT ON THE FAIR NAME OF RAJPUTANA, – GO AND DROWN YOURSELF IN SOME RIVER!!!

MIRA, THE TRUE HINDU WIFE, DID NOT PROTEST. SHE FONDLY TOOK LEAVE OF HER TEARFUL COMPANIONS...

... AND SLOWLY WENDED HER WAY TO THE RIVER, HUGGING THE IMAGE OF HER LORD CLOSE TO HER.

AS MIRA STOOD ON THE RIVER-BANK, THE TEMPLE BELLS CHIMED.
SHE WAS ABOUT TO JUMP, WHEN A HAND FROM BEHIND
GRASPED HER. SHE TURNED AROUND...

...AND WHAT SHOULD MEET HER EYES BUT THE HEAVENLY SMILE OF HER BELOVED LORD! SHE FAINTED.

WHEN MIRA REGAINED CONSCIOUSNESS—

YOUR LIFE WITH YOUR HUSBAND IS OVER. NOW YOU ARE MINE. GO AND SEEK ME HENCEFORTH IN BRINDAVAN.

MY LORD! MY LORD!

AFTER RECEIVING THE DIVINE COMMAND, MIRA SANG AND DANCED HER WAY TO BRINDAVAN, HARDLY AWARE OF ALL THAT SHE HAD TO SUFFER ON THE WAY.

GOPALA, YOU ARE ALL I HAVE AND NONE ELSE! AND I AM THE HAPPIER FOR IT!

AT LAST SHE REACHED HER DESTINATION— BRINDAVAN.

HARDLY HAD SHE ARRIVED WHEN DEVOTEES BEGAN TO FLOCK AROUND HER.

NEWS SPREAD THAT MIRA HAD COME.

MIRA HAS COME!

HAVE YOU HEARD HER SING TO GOPALA?

IT SEEMED AS IF HER DEVOTEES HAD HEARD OF HER AND WERE WAITING FOR HER.

GOPALA HAS SENT HER AT LAST!

SHE IS RADHA REBORN!

ONCE MORE THERE WILL BE SINGING AND DANCING IN BRINDAVAN!

PEOPLE CAME FROM FAR OFF PLACES TO HAVE A GLIMPSE OF THIS UNINHIBITED DEVOTEE OF LORD KRISHNA. ONE OF THEM WAS A TRAVELLER FROM CHITTOR!

MIRABAI ALIVE!! I MUST TAKE THIS NEWS TO RANA BHOJRAJ!

WHEN HE RETURNED TO CHITTOR—

OUR PRINCESS IS ALIVE, YOUR HIGHNESS!

WHAT!!

IT CANNOT BE! I HAVE BEEN GIVEN ANOTHER CHANCE!

AFTER MIRA HAD GONE TO OBEY HIS COMMAND, BHOJRAJ HAD REPENTED OF HIS HARSH SENTENCE.

MIRA IS ALIVE!! I WILL GO TO HER AND BEG HER FORGIVENESS.

DRESSED IN THE SAFFRON ROBES OF A SADHU, BHOJRAJ TRAVELLED TO BRINDAVAN. HE APPROACHED MIRA AND HELD OUT HIS PALM —

WHAT CAN I, WHO AM A BEGGAR, GIVE YOU?

YOU CAN GIVE ME ALL THAT I WANT NOW OF LIFE!

SUDDENLY, BHOJRAJ THREW OFF HIS SAFFRON ROBES AND MIRA, RECOGNISING HER HUSBAND, FELL AT HIS FEET.

I BEG YOUR FORGIVENESS, MIRA, THAT IS ALL I BEG. PLEASE COME TO CHITTOR.

HAS MIRA EVER GONE AGAINST THE WISHES OF HER HUSBAND? YES, I WILL COME TO CHITTOR!

SO MIRA, LED BY HER HUSBAND AND FOLLOWED BY HER DEVOTEES, RETURNED TO CHITTOR.

HE WOULD NOT GIVE ME GLORY, POWER, WEALTH OR FAME, BUT ONLY HIS LOVE'S ROSARY, AND SAID: "SING, SING MY NAME!"

AT CHITTOR, FOR MANY YEARS, SHE CONTINUED HER WORSHIP OF HER LORD, WITH COMPLETE FREEDOM.

KEEP AWAY FROM EVIL COMPANY. EMPTY YOUR MINDS OF JEALOUSY, GREED, ATTACHMENT AND PRIDE...

ALMOST TEN YEARS HAD PASSED SINCE MIRA HAD FIRST ARRIVED — AS BHOU-RAJ'S BRIDE— TO CHITTOR, WHEN ALAS! SHE WAS WIDOWED!

BHOURAJ'S FATHER SUMMONED MIRA.

PREPARE YOURSELF FOR SATI! YOU MUST JOIN YOUR HUSBAND ON THE FUNERAL PYRE!

BUT MIRA REFUSED.

AS LONG AS THE DIVINE LORD LIVES IN MY HEART, I WILL NOT DIE!

THOUGH THE WIDOWED MIRA WAS NOW MORALLY FREE TO DEVOTE HERSELF COMPLETELY TO HER LORD, THE NEW RANA, BHOURAJ'S BROTHER, GAVE HER NO PEACE.

I COMMAND YOU HENCE-FORTH NOT TO MIX WITH HOLY MEN AND NOT TO SING AND DANCE BEFORE THE IMAGE OF KRISHNA WITHIN THE WALLS OF THIS PALACE!

MIRA WAS RESTLESS AND UNHAPPY—

O GOPALA! IF I CANNOT WORSHIP YOU IN PEACE IN THE PALACE TEMPLE, I WILL GO TO THE PUBLIC TEMPLE!

SO THERE SHE WENT.

BUT NOW THE RANA RIDICULED HER FOR MINGLING SHAMELESSLY WITH THE SADHUS AND THE COMMON DEVOTEES.

YOU REFUSED TO JOIN YOUR HUSBAND ON THE FUNERAL PYRE!! WAS IT ONLY TO REVEL IN THE COMPANY OF THESE BEGGARS?

MIRA IGNORED THESE TAUNTS AND CONTINUED SINGING AND DANCING IN THE NAME OF HER LORD.

GOPALA IS MY BELOVED! MIRA'S LORD IS GOPALA!

THE PEOPLE OF CHITTOR BEGAN TO LOVE AND RESPECT THEIR SAINTLY PRINCESS EVEN MORE, AND NEWS ABOUT HER SPREAD ALL OVER INDIA.

SCHOLARS AND SAINTS OF HER TIME CAME FROM DISTANT PLACES TO PAY HOMAGE TO HER.

MEDITATE ON THE FEET OF THE LORD. FASTS, PILGRIMAGES AND LEARNING ARE OF NO USE. LOVE THE LORD WITH ALL YOUR MIND AND HEART.

THE RANA WAS NOW BESIDE HIMSELF WITH RAGE.

SOMEHOW WE MUST GET RID OF THIS WICKED WOMAN WHO CASTS HER SPELL OVER ALL WHO COME HER WAY!

BUT MIRA'S DEVOTION WAS UNSHAKEN AND SHE CONTINUED HER SINGING AND DANCING IN THE NAME OF HER LORD.

ONE DAY THE RANA HAD A BASKET, CONTAINING A POISONOUS SNAKE, SENT TO HER.

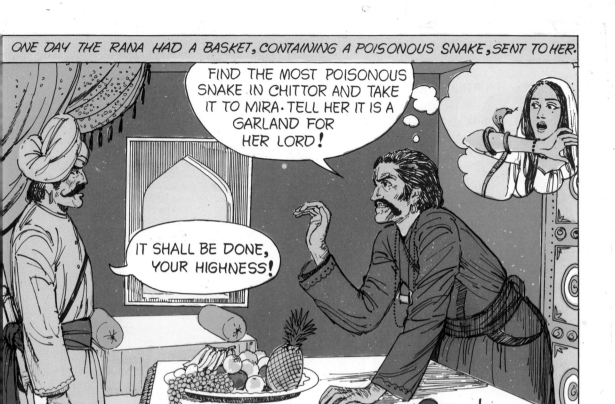

FIND THE MOST POISONOUS SNAKE IN CHITTOR AND TAKE IT TO MIRA. TELL HER IT IS A GARLAND FOR HER LORD!

IT SHALL BE DONE, YOUR HIGHNESS!

MIRA NEVER REFUSED ANYTHING THAT WAS GIVEN IN THE NAME OF HER LORD.

I WILL ACCEPT ANYTHING OFFERED FOR THE WORSHIP OF MY LORD.

AND WHEN MIRA OPENED THE BASKET, LO! THE SNAKE HAD INDEED BECOME A GARLAND.

SHE GARLANDED HER LORD'S IMAGE AND THANKED THE ASTONISHED MESSENGER!

MY ACKNOWLEDGEMENT AND THANKS TO THE RANA FOR HIS KIND GESTURE.

ON ANOTHER DAY—

REMOVE MIRA'S BED-STEAD. REPLACE IT WITH ANOTHER OF POISON-TIPPED NAILS! CONCEAL THE NAILS WITH ROSE PETALS!

IT SHALL BE DONE, YOUR HIGHNESS!

MIRA, HARDLY CONSCIOUS OF ANY CHANGE IN HER SURROUNDINGS, LAY DOWN AS USUAL. MIRACULOUSLY, THE NAILS TURNED LIMP AND SOFT LIKE THE VERY ROSE PETALS THAT COVERED THEM!!!

AND MIRA SLEPT PEACEFULLY THE WHOLE NIGHT THROUGH, DREAMING OF HER LORD...

GOPALA IS MY LORD. HE PROTECTS ME FROM ALL ONSLAUGHTS. NO ONE WILL PREVENT ME FROM WORSHIPPING MY LORD.

THE RANA NOW WAS FURIOUS. HE MIXED POISON INTO A BOWL OF NECTAR WITH HIS OWN HANDS.

I WILL MAKE CERTAIN MIRA DOES NOT ESCAPE THIS TIME!!

HE SENT FOR HIS MOST TRUSTED MAN.

TAKE THIS BOWL OF NECTAR TO MIRA AND — BE SURE SHE DRINKS IT IN YOUR PRESENCE!!

THE MAN TOOK THE BOWL TO MIRA.

A BOWL OF NECTAR FROM THE RANA WHO REPENTS OF HIS HARSH TREATMENT OF MIRABAI.

MIRA, HARDLY CONSCIOUS OF WHAT SHE ATE OR DRANK, ACCEPTED THE NECTAR AND SWALLOWED IT MECHANICALLY.

AND LO! THE POISON TURNED INTO NECTAR!!

MIRA IS UNAFFECTED!! I CAN'T BELIEVE MY EYES!

MIRA CONTINUED SITTING BEFORE HER LORD WITH A SMILE ON HER LIPS.

THE FRUSTRATED RANA FINALLY DECIDED TO HARASS MIRA INTO GIVING UP.

MIRA MUST NOT ENTER THE PUBLIC TEMPLE. HER IMMODESTY BRINGS SHAME UPON THE FAIR NAME OF OUR ROYAL FAMILY!

IT WILL BE SEEN TO, YOUR HIGHNESS!

MIRA WAS TIRED OF THESE CEASELESS INTERRUPTIONS.

O GOPALA, WILL THEY NEVER LEAVE ME IN PEACE TO ADORE YOU? WHAT SHOULD I DO?

SHE WROTE TO TULSIDAS, A SAINT OF HER TIMES, AND ASKED HIM WHAT SHE SHOULD DO.

I WILL ACT ON THE SAINT'S ADVICE. HE IS WISE AND LOVES MY LORD AS I DO.

TULSIDAS ADVISES ME TO SHUN THOSE WHO COME IN THE WAY OF MY WORSHIP EVEN THOUGH THEY BE MY CLOSEST RELATIVES

MIRA TOOK THE HINT AND LEFT CHITTOR FOR MERTA, HER UNCLE'S KINGDOM. THERE SHE WAS LOVINGLY WELCOMED.

SHE WAS GIVEN FULL FREEDOM TO WORSHIP IN PEACE.

AND SO SHE PASSED A FEW MORE YEARS IMMERSED IN HER LORD.

MIRA WAS GROWING OLD. SHE KNEW THAT HER END WAS NEAR.

MY LORD, IT IS TIME YOU TOOK ME TO YOU AND TO REST. I SHALL VISIT ALL THE PLACES DEAR TO YOU AND THEN WAIT FOR YOU.

SO SHE SET OUT ON A PILGRIMAGE TO MATHURA...

EVERLASTINGLY I WILL CHASE YOU— A SHADOW LOYAL AND TRUE, AND WILL RECEIVE WHATEVER YOU GIVE ME

···BRINDAVAN ···

MY HEART SINGS: YOU ARE CLOSER THAN ALL· MY QUEST, MY HOPE, MY BREATH, MY LIGHT, MY ONLY REFUGE, LIFE'S ONE CALL, MY SOUL'S ONE YEARNING—DAY AND NIGHT!

···AND DWARKA ·

NOW MIRA IS OBLIVIOUS TO THE WORLD. BUT SINGS AND SINGS AND SINGS: MY BELOVED'S COME TO ME!

SHE STAYED ON AT DWARKA BECAUSE THE CALL OF HER LORD HAD BECOME LOUDER AND MORE INSISTENT.

IT IS FOR YOU TO ORDAIN NOW, MY DESTINY— ONLY YOU KNOW HOW TO MAKE ME YOUR OWN.

ONE DAY IN THE MIDDLE OF A PRAYER MEETING THE CALL CAME SO LOUD AND DEAFENING THAT MIRA, WHILE DANCING FELL INTO A TRANCE AND FAINTED ON HER LORD.

I HAVE SURRENDERED MYSELF TO YOU. TILL MY LAST BREATH I'LL STAND AT YOUR DOOR, ACCEPTING ALL, LORD— LIFE OR DEATH.

AND MIRA AT LAST BECAME ONE WITH THE LORD SHE HAD WORSHIPPED AND YEARNED FOR, EVER SINCE SHE HAD TAKEN HIM FOR HER BRIDEGROOM, AT THE TENDER AGE OF FIVE !!